gto

THE YOUNGEST SHEPHERD

A TALE OF THE NATIVITY

by Hal Borland

Drawings by Peter Burchard

This beautiful story of a boy, an old man and a bird on the first Christmas Eve is a new expression of the triumphant joy and wonder of the Nativity. The boy and the old man were among the shepherds who were grazing their sheep on the hills above Bethlehem; the bird, a voiceless little thrush which was also touched by the miracle of the Saviour's birth.

Into his story of what happened that memorable night, the author has woven fragments of several ancient legends; and he has carefully reconstructed the landscape and nomadic life of Palestine as they must have been nearly two thousand years ago. *The Youngest Shepherd* vividly evokes the time, place and spirit of the first Christmas, and readers of all ages will take it to their hearts for many Christmases to come.

THE

YOUNGEST

SHEPHERD

THE
YOUNGEST
SHEPHERD

A TALE OF THE NATIVITY

BY HAL BORLAND

DRAWINGS BY PETER BURCHARD

J. B. LIPPINCOTT COMPANY
PHILADELPHIA AND NEW YORK

FOR BARBARA

THE shepherd with the coarse red beard was a practical man. He listened to the patriarch of the little group around the fire, and he asked, "Did they have better flocks than ours in Egypt?"

The patriarch fingered his white beard and drew his worn robe closer about him, for it was one of those cold, clear nights that come to the hill country when the days are at their shortest. He shook his head. "Their rams were big, but their ewes had poor fleece. It takes hill country to grow good wool. Cold nights make warm cloth."

The youngest of the half-dozen shepherds, a boy of perhaps fourteen, had listened with glowing eyes to the old man's tales of his long-ago trip to Egypt. "Tell us about the cities of Egypt," he urged.

"I saw no cities," the old man said. "We took the flock to a market town like Bethlehem, yonder. The townspeople were like us, humble and tax-ridden."

"Taxes!" The red-bearded one scowled at the fire. Taxes were a sore point with all of them, for they had just been summoned to Bethlehem, their ancestral home, to pay a levy set by Augustus Caesar in far-off Rome. Bethlehem was crowded with taxpayers.

The old man said, "Taxes are always levied. Why else are there so many poor? Foreign kings spend all their days thinking up taxes."

"Did you see the kings of Egypt?" the boy asked eagerly.

"No, my son," the old man said.

"I wish I might see a king!" the boy exclaimed. "Just to see a king would be wondrous!"

"Perhaps you shall," the patriarch said. "We shall have our own king again. The prophets have said—"

"I have heard that all my years," the red-bearded one interrupted. "We had our kings." He glanced at the boy, amused. "A king would hold his nose at sight of you. You're like the rest of us. You smell of the flock. Kings!" He laughed wryly.

"David tended flock," the old man reminded him. He shifted a lame leg painfully, edged toward the fire. "David was the son of Jesse, who dwelt yonder, in Bethlehem. David knew these hills, perhaps sat as you, my son, beside such a fire as this on this very hilltop."

And the red-bearded one said, "David is dead a long, long time."

8

THE group fell silent. The beardless boy sat staring at the fire, thinking of David, the legendary one, who tended flock even as he, and who slew a giant while still a boy, and sang songs, and who was a great king among his people. The old tales ran through his mind, and his face was aglow with the oft-told stories.

They sat in silence, and the night wind had a nip. The man with a red beard said to the boy, "Go see to the flocks," and the boy roused, as from a trance, and got to his feet and left the fire. He went to the hollow nearby, watching the stars overhead and curling his sandaled toes against the icy dew on the grass underfoot.

The sheep were sleeping, each flock lying close to share the huddled warmth. He turned back toward the fire to warm himself again. Then the night wind stilled.

There was a rush as of great wings, and suddenly a strange light bathed the whole hilltop. The shepherds at the fire looked up, startled, and the red-bearded one leaped to his feet in alarm.

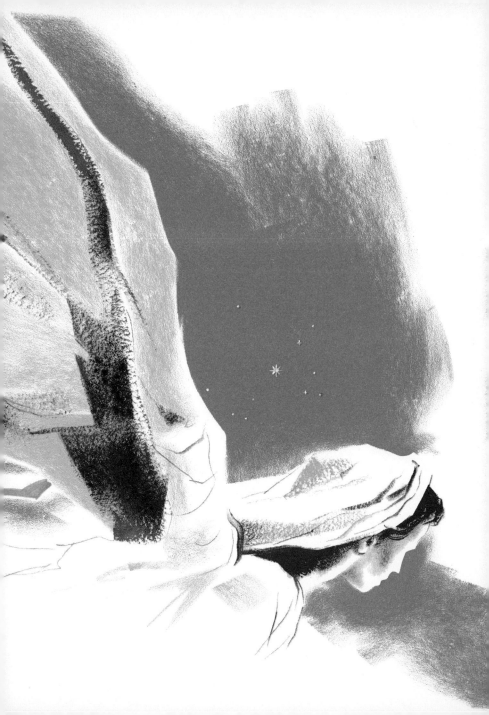

The boy heard a voice saying, "Fear not: for, behold, I bring you good tidings of great joy, which shall be to all people. For unto you is born this day in the city of David a Saviour, which is Christ the Lord. And this shall be a sign unto you; Ye shall find the babe wrapped in swaddling clothes, lying in a manger."

And there was the sound of praise and song and great joy.

The light faded and the shepherds looked at one another in awe. The boy whispered, "A Saviour, a King!" And he said aloud, "We must go and see this!"

But the shepherd with the red beard said, "This is no matter for young boys." He looked around at the others. "This could be another trick of the tax collectors."

"This is no trick," the old man said quietly. "This is the prophecies come true. We must go down to Bethlehem, the city of David, and see this thing which is come to pass and which the Lord has made known to us. The Lord our God does not play tricks."

"We shall see," the red-bearded one said. He turned to the boy. "You stay and watch the flocks." Then he said to the others, "Come, let us go."

The old man saw the look on the boy's face. "Go, my son," he said. "Go and see. I shall stay and watch the flocks."

So they went, hurrying toward a star that now stood over Bethlehem, and the old man limped around the flocks, saw the sheep huddled and content. He returned to the fire, thrust a fresh fagot into the coals, drew his worn robe about him and sat down.

He told himself that his king was the God of Abraham and, since he was full of years, he would soon be gathered to his fathers and would see Him face to face. He drowsed, and he dreamed of music and an angel, and of Abraham himself. He wakened and quoted the old words: "Your old men shall dream dreams, your young men shall see visions." And he said to himself, "Surely the God of Abraham will understand why I did not go. Surely He will understand and forgive."

As the shepherds went down from the hilltop in the starlit night a small red-brown bird with a gray breast came and perched on the boy's shoulder. The boy, his heart full of wonder and belief, tried to tell the bird why they were going down to Bethlehem. "Have you ever seen a king, brown bird?" he asked.

The bird made no answer.

The other shepherds smiled. The one with a red beard said, "Fool! Do you not know the voiceless thrush when it is right before your eyes? You ask it to speak, the bird that cannot even twitter!" He laughed aloud.

The boy said nothing more to the bird.

They went down the hillside and crossed the valley, with its shadowy olive groves. They went up the slope to Bethlehem and passed the inn, which was loud with voices and laughter. Beyond the inn, on the hillside, they came to the stable and went in, as they had been bidden.

In the stable the boy saw the oxen kneeling, and he smelled the sweetness of fresh flowers newly come to blossom in the hay. And there in a manger he saw a newborn babe. He heard the great chorus of praise and hallelujah that filled the sky, the air and the stable itself. He knew that this babe in swaddling clothes was the Saviour, the King who was to come to his people.

The boy's heart began to sing. He turned to the bird, still there on his shoulder, and he whispered, "Sing! Rejoice!"

The bird opened its beak, but no sound came.

"Make a joyful noise, brown bird!" the boy urged.

And still the bird could make no song.

A third time the boy urged. "Sing! Sing as the angels sing!"

And the bird sang. It flew about the stable singing, and it went out into the night and sang as the angels sang.

22

IN the darkness just before dawn they started back to their flocks on the hilltop. As the night thinned away and the stars dimmed, they hurried, knowing the flocks would soon leave their bed-ground. The old man, lame as he was, might have trouble holding the flocks apart in their hungry grazing. They always grazed hungrily in early morning, for the dew-wet grass provided most of their water in this scantly watered land.

Hurrying, the boy scuffed a pebble into his sandal, but he was loath to stop and lag behind the others. He limped painfully, keeping up, till they came to a level place halfway up the hill. There he paused and took off his sandal. As he removed the pebble, the sun rose. He looked back in the dazzling light, thinking there had never before been a morning like this. He could see the five roads that came to a crossing near the inn in Bethlehem. He could see the inn. But he could not see the stable, it was so small and so hidden among the rocks.

He put on his sandal again and tied the thongs and ran to catch up with the others.

The sun was half-an-hour high when the shepherds returned to the fire on the hilltop. The flocks were grazing well apart, and the old man stood waiting, leaning on his staff, his beard frosty white and his eyes asking questions.

One shepherd said, "We went as we were bidden. In the stable, in a manger, we saw a babe."

"In swaddling clothes," another said, "just as the angel told us!" His voice was hushed.

Still another said, "The oxen knelt in adoration!"

The red-bearded one spoke up impatiently. "All oxen kneel when they rise from their beds. That has no importance. Even our own sheep kneel when they are getting to their feet."

Another said, "The voiceless thrush began to sing, right there in the stable! There were many miracles."

The red-bearded one turned to him and asked sharply, "Was it the bird who sang, or the boy?" Then he glanced at the old man. "I was almost persuaded," he said, "and yet. . . ." He shook his head, puzzling. He turned and looked toward Bethlehem, so small there on the low hilltop beyond the valley. "If a great thing were to happen," he demanded, "why should it happen in such a crossroads village? Nothing important has happened in Bethlehem in a thousand years!"

Then he looked toward the north. In the bright, clear light of morning all could see the distant shimmer of the walls and towers of the city where David ruled long ago and where Solomon once built his great temple. The red-bearded one thrust out a hairy hand, pointing. "There, in Jerusalem," he said, "is where our kings ruled—when we had kings! There is the center of our priesthood, our laws, our faith." He turned to the others. "Did you note that there was not a priest at the stable, not one?"

The old man said quietly, "True, Jerusalem is the center of the priesthood. But it is not the center of our faith. Our faith is in our hearts." He looked away, toward the humble village. "If a great thing were to happen for simple folk, like us," he said, "surely it could happen in a simple place, like Bethlehem." He searched their faces, and his eyes sought out the boy, to ask a question.

The boy stood a few steps apart from the others. He had not spoken, and now his face was turned to the sky. All followed his look and saw the brown bird fly down and perch on the boy's shoulder. He smiled at the bird, and he whispered to it. And the bird flew from his shoulder, singing as it rose in the air, singing a wondrous song as of angels singing.

The old man, seeing the wonder and exaltation in the boy's face, knew there was no need for his question.

Then, in the awed silence among them, one shepherd whispered, "For the boy, this voiceless bird is become a nightingale."